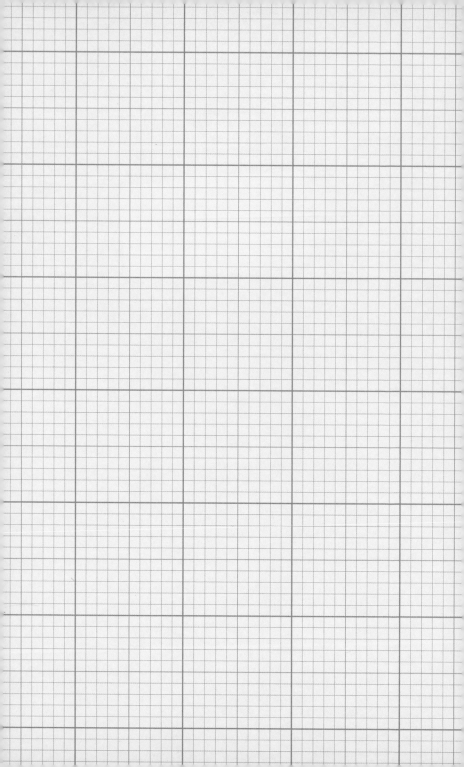

Sofia

THE QUESTIONEERS

SOFIA VALDEZ

AND THE VANISHING VOTE

by Andrea Beaty

illustrations by David Roberts

AMULET BOOKS

NEW YORK

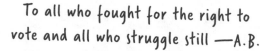

To all who fought for the right to vote and all who struggle still —A.B.

Cataloging-in-Publication Data has been applied for and may be obtained from the Library of Congress.

ISBN 978-1-4197-4350-4

Text copyright © 2020 Andrea Beaty
Illustrations copyright © 2020 David Roberts
Book design by Marcie J. Lawrence

Printed and bound in USA
10 9 8 7 6 5 4 3 2

Amulet Books are available at special discounts when purchased in quantity for premiums and promotions as well as fundraising or educational use. Special editions can also be created to specification. For details, contact specialsales@abramsbooks.com or the address below.

ABRAMS The Art of Books
195 Broadway, New York, NY 10007
abramsbooks.com

CHAPTER 1

Sofia rushed around the house looking for her red shoe.

"Please hurry, Abuelo! I can't be late today!" she said.

Abuelo calmly looked up from the lunch he was packing.

"Sofia. Do I ever make you late to school?" he asked, raising his left eyebrow just so.

It was Abuelo's *why don't you think about that for a moment* look. Abuelo had a look for every situation, and Sofia knew them all by heart. They were always kind, but they got their message through. Abuelo didn't have to say a lot to say a lot.

"I know," said Sofia. "But I really can't be late today. Miss Greer has a surprise for us!"

Abuelo smiled at his granddaughter. "Here's a surprise," he said. "Your shoe is under the couch."

"I should have known," said Sofia, looking at Pup.

Pup barked and wagged his tail. He fetched his leash and ran to the door. He was ready to go. A few minutes later, they were on their way.

Sofia, Abuelo, and Pup walked to Blue River Creek Elementary School together every day. Today, Sofia couldn't stop wondering about the surprise her teacher, Miss Lila Greer, had in store for her second-grade class.

"Maybe it's a field trip!" said Sofia. "The last one was so exciting. The bridge collapsed and

Miss Greer got stuck on an island. Then, Iggy showed us how to make a new bridge with shoelaces and Fruit Roll-Ups. It was cool. Miss Greer said that was a Learning Experience."

"That's for sure," said Abuelo.

"Maybe it's an experiment!" said Sofia. "Last time, Ada taught us about chemistry and how to make rainbow geysers. I don't think Miss Greer liked the mess, but she said it was a Learning Experience, too."

"That would be one," Abuelo said with a chuckle.

Sofia thought a moment.

"We sure have a lot of Learning Experiences in second grade," she said.

"You surely do," said Abuelo.

They reached the school, and Sofia scratched Pup's ear.

Abuelo handed her the lunch bag. "Extra cookies today," he said. "For sharing."

Abuelo always packed extra cookies for sharing. It was one of the things Sofia loved about him. It was one of the things her friends loved, too. Abuelo was the best baker in Blue River Creek. For years, his bakery, La Panaderia de la Magnolia, was the most popular place in town for people to gather for coffee and cookies and Mexican sweet breads. He was famous for his pan dulce. Abuelo was retired now, but he still baked for Sofia and her friends and anyone else who might need a treat. He was kind like that.

"Te amo," Sofia said.

"Mi vida," said Abuelo, hugging her tight.

Sofia hugged him back, then she ran through the open school door, ready for the big surprise.

CHAPTER 2

"What do you think the surprise will be?" asked Rosie Revere, who sat next to Sofia. "I hope we're engineering again. That was so much fun. But I don't think Miss Greer liked it when we made inventions and the log scooter knocked Iggy's apartment-building-slash-airplane into the ant farm. What did she call it when we were trying to catch the ants?"

"A Learning Experience," said Ada, plopping

down next to them. "She says that a lot. Do you think that's a good thing?"

Before Sofia could answer, Miss Greer entered the classroom.

"Good morning!" she said. "As you know, I have a surprise announcement for you." Miss Greer silently waited for all her students to look at her. That was how she got their attention without a lot of fuss. It worked. Within seconds, everyone was sitting quietly with their mouths closed and their eyes open.

"Thank you, class," said Miss Greer. "As you know, second grade is a time for new experiences. And responsibilities." She paused and looked at the students seriously.

"I believe that you are ready for a very big responsibility."

"Like a chore?" someone asked.

"Yes, but a good one," said Miss Greer. "I think we should get a class pet!"

The class cheered.

"We will raise money to buy the pet and feed it. Everyone will take turns caring for the pet. So it will be a big responsibility," she said. "What kind should we get?"

Immediately, the class erupted with ideas.

"A pony!"

"A buffalo!"

"A giraffe!"

"Oh . . ." Miss Greer said. "Hmm. Well . . ."

"A boa constrictor!"

"Hot dogs!"

"A giant squid!"

"A giant one?" Miss Greer asked. She looked worried.

"A killer shark!"

Miss Greer looked a little dizzy and started to sway. The last time she looked like that was when she fainted on the island during their field trip.

"Are you okay, Miss Greer?" asked Iggy.

"Oh dear," said Miss Greer, imagining giant squids and killer sharks eating hot dogs in her classroom.

"Killer squids and giant sharks," she mumbled.

"We could get a small one," said Rosie.

"A small shark?" asked Miss Greer.

"No," said Rosie. "A small pet."

Miss Greer perked up. "That's a good idea," she said, pointing to a low bookcase by the window. "The pet's home will be on top of that bookcase. So, no giant squids."

"Aw, rats," said someone in the back.

"Rats?" said Miss Greer with her eyes wide open. "Oh, double dear . . . No rats!"

"A yeti!"

"It has to be small," said Miss Greer.

"A small yeti."

"Oh, triple dear!" said Miss Greer, plopping into her seat. "I thought this would be easy. Maybe we're not ready to choose a pet."

"We can do it!" said Rosie.

"But everyone wants a different thing," said Miss Greer. "How can we possibly pick one good pet for a class of seventeen different students?"

Sofia Valdez jumped to her feet. "I know!" she cried.

Everyone turned to look at Sofia. They all leaned toward her, and she leaned back just a bit. She felt nervous. Then she remembered the time she went to City Hall and had to be brave and talk to the mayor and the whole city government and ask them to build a park. That had been very scary.

She looked at the smiling faces of her friends in Grade Two and at her slightly worried teacher. This was not so scary. Sofia smiled and raised her head high.

"I know how to do it," she repeated. "Let's have an election!"

Miss Greer clapped her hands. "What a perfect idea!" she said. "Everyone, go home tonight and make a poster for the pet you would like to nominate. Remember, it has to fit on the bookcase!"

The class cheered.

"Tomorrow, we'll vote," said Miss Greer. "An election is the perfect way to decide. There's nothing complicated about that! It will be easy!"

After school, Sofia met Abuelo and Pup by the flagpole. All around them, students were talking about the election and the pets they would nominate. Sofia hugged Abuelo, and they walked home together quietly. Sofia was deep in thought. Something was bugging her.

"What's wrong, Sofia?" asked Abuelo. "You

haven't said a single word since we left school. Did something happen?"

"We're going to elect a class pet," said Sofia.

"That sounds like a good thing," said Abuelo. "Aren't you happy?"

Sofia thought for a moment.

"I am," she said. "But Miss Greer said something else. She said it would be easy. You've told me lots of stories about elections that were really hard."

Abuelo pulled a cookie from his pocket and gave it to Sofia. He pulled out another and sneaked a pinch to Pup.

"I've seen a lot of elections in my time," said Abuelo. "And I've never seen an easy one. But that's okay. Important things are worth the hard work."

Sofia frowned. "I think," she said, "this might be what Miss Greer calls a real Learning Experience."

"Maybe," said Abuelo. "But maybe it will turn out like this batch of cookies."

"What do you mean?" asked Sofia.

"Maybe . . ." said Abuelo with a grin, "it will be a good one!"

CHAPTER 3

That night, Sofia's friends came over to make posters at the kitchen table. Abuelo came in every few minutes to check the oven. He was making orejas, which were one of Sofia's favorite treats. Abuelo had worked all afternoon preparing the smooth dough. He rolled, folded, and chilled the dough over and over. He sprinkled the final layers with cane sugar and cinnamon before he sliced and baked the cookies. It took a lot of time to make the sweet, flaky dough, so Abuelo did not make them very often, and it was always a special treat when he did.

"We'll give some to Marisella to celebrate her new baby brother," said Abuelo.

Marisella was Sofia's third-grade cousin, whose baby brother was only three weeks old.

"She'll love that, Abuelo," said Sofia.

The smell of sweet pastries filled the air as Ada, Rosie, Sofia, and Iggy brainstormed ideas for the best class pet.

"I'm voting for a turtle or maybe a lemur," said Ada. "Or a flying squirrel. Do they really fly? Can they fly upside down?"

"I'm picking a bird," said Rosie. "I love my bird, Gizmo, and Aunt Rose's bird, Gadget. Plus, birds know how to make things, just like engineers. Could you make a nest with only a beak and your feet?"

"What about you, Iggy?" asked Sofia.

Iggy proudly showed them the poster he had been working on.

"It's a building," said Sofia. "Buildings can't be pets."

"Why not?" asked Iggy. "You don't have to take it for walks or clean its cage. It's perfect."

"It's too big," said Ada.

"I'll make a model," said Iggy. "I can make models from anything."

That was true. Iggy had once made a model of the St. Louis Arch from pancakes and coconut pie. It was beautiful and delicious.

"What about you, Sofia?" asked Rosie.

"I can't decide," she said. "There are so many choices, but not a perfect one. They all have something good and something bad about them."

"You don't have to find the perfect pet," said Abuelo. "Just the best one."

Sofia thought about that. She was always trying to make things better. Sometimes, she worried too much about making them perfect.

There was never a perfect candidate in an election. How could there be? People aren't perfect. Maybe it was the same with pets. After all, how could one pet be perfect for everyone? What pet would be good for as many kids as possible?

Abuelo checked the oven once more. "Aha!" he said, pulling out the cookie tray. "This is a batch to be proud of."

He put the orejas on a plate in front of the Questioneers and brought the kids cups of hot chocolate.

"Thank you, Mr. Valdez!" said Ada.

"What does *orejas* mean?" asked Rosie.

"*Ears*," said Sofia.

"Wait," said Abuelo. "I can't hear you."

He held one of the curvy pastries up to his head like it was a sugar-covered ear.

"That's better," he said. "Can you repeat the question?"

Abuelo winked at Sofia. Then he took a bite of the pastry.

"Ouch!" he cried. "My ear hurts!"

Ada, Iggy, and Rosie laughed. Sofia couldn't help laughing, too. Abuelo had been telling her that joke since she was a baby. He had lots of jokes like that. Sofia could always count on him to tell them. It was one of the things she loved most about Abuelo—that she could always count on him.

Ada held up one of the orejas and rotated it. "Look!" she said. "This way, it looks like a butterfly."

Sofia smiled. "That's it! I'll nominate a butterfly! Everyone loves butterflies!"

CHAPTER 4

The next day, Miss Greer's class learned about the candidates. One by one, the students gave short speeches about their nominees. The presentations lasted until lunch. Then, after recess, it was finally election time!

"Write your vote on a slip of paper, and put it in this ballot box," said Miss Greer. "The pet with the most votes wins."

After the voting, Miss Greer counted the votes and wrote the nominees on the board.

"One vote for aardvark," she said. "One for butterfly. One for turtle. One for miniature giraffe? One for . . ."

Finally, Miss Greer pulled the last ballot from the box. "Last vote . . . goes to a skunk? Oh, dear! Well, let's see who won."

She stepped back from the board and frowned. Each pet had exactly one vote. Every student had voted for the pet they had nominated.

There were seventeen winners, but there could only be one pet.

"Oh dear," said Miss Greer. "We can't have seventeen pets!"

"Why don't we do it like elections for the president?" asked Sofia. "We could have an election to find the top two candidates. That's called a primary election. Then we'll vote for one of the top two in order to pick the class pet."

"Wouldn't everyone just vote for their own choices again?" asked Ada.

"Hmm," said Miss Greer. "First, we need to adjust the requirements. Some of these nominees have very sharp teeth. And we can't have a pet someone is allergic to. Imagine the sneezing!

How could we get any work done? We don't want a stinky pet. Or a noisy one!"

"Most elections have rules for the candidates," said Sofia. "American presidents have to be at least thirty-five years old and must have been a U.S. citizen since they were born. And they must have lived in the country for at least fourteen years."

"I don't think those rules will work for pets," said Iggy. "Animals aren't citizens, are they?"

"Some animals don't even live fourteen years. But some live a lot longer," said Ada. "African elephants can live over seventy years. And Greenland sharks can live two hundred seventy-five years!"

"Sharks?!" said Miss Greer.

"And eels can live for decades," said Ada. "And lay millions of eggs! Zowie!"

"Millions of eggs?!" Miss Greer said.

Miss Greer plopped into her seat. She looked queasy for a moment. Then, she shook it off, patted her hair neatly back into place, and stood up.

"It will be okay," she said. "It will be okay."

"Is she talking to us?" Ada whispered to Iggy.

"I don't think so," Iggy whispered back.

"Perhaps . . ." said Miss Greer. "Perhaps we should make a list of requirements."

She erased the board and started a list.

The students made suggestions, and soon the list was complete.

Miss Greer stood back and smiled.

"There," she said. "That seems reasonable."

List of Requirements for Class Pet Candidates

- Does not stink
- Does not bite
- Does not eat students
- Does not cause sneezing
- Is not poisonous
- Is big enough to see
- Is small enough to fit on bookcase
- Is not named "Geraldine"
- Is not extinct
- Does not lay millions of eggs

List of Candidates

1. ~~Sea Horse~~
2. Turtle ✓
3. ~~Aardvark~~
4. ~~Miniature Giraffe~~
5. Chrysler Building ✓
6. ~~Baby shark~~
7. ~~Mama shark~~
8. Bird ✓
9. ~~Small Yeti~~
10. ~~Skunk~~
11. Fish ✓
12. Lizard ✓
13. ~~Butterfly~~
14. ~~Ostrich~~
15. ~~Mongoose~~
16. ~~Monkey~~
17. ~~Hyena~~

CHAPTER 5

The class compared the list of candidates against the requirements. One by one, they crossed candidates off the list.

"What about this one?" asked Miss Greer, pointing to the Chrysler Building. "It's not poisonous, and it's not going to bite anyone."

"It's not named Geraldine!" said Ada.

"It fits all the requirements," said Rosie.

"Then it's in!" said Miss Greer, smiling at Iggy. Iggy Peck smiled back.

"Okay," said Miss Greer. "Let's vote again."

Miss Greer tallied the votes.

Turtle—5

Bird—6

Lizard—3

Fish—2

Chrysler Building—1

"There we have it," said Miss Greer. "Turtle and Bird. Our two candidates."

Sofia smiled. Things were going so well. She could imagine real presidential candidates having conversations just like this one. Only without skunks and giraffes. What if the class could make this choice even more like a real election?

"Miss Greer?" said Sofia. "I've been thinking. Can we do this just like a real presidential election? Can we have campaigns and everything?"

Miss Greer thought for a moment.

"That's a good idea," said Miss Greer. "And since it was your idea, Sofia, you should be the election commissioner."

"What's an election commissioner?" asked Iggy.

"The commissioner makes sure the election is fair and that everybody's right to vote is protected," said Miss Greer. "They make the ballots and run the election. It's a difficult but very important job. The election commissioner promises to follow the rules and be fair."

"I can do that," said Sofia. "I promise."

Miss Greer smiled. "Rosie will run the Bird campaign since it was her nominee," she said. "And Ada will run the campaign for Turtle for the same reason."

"What about everyone else?" asked someone in the back of the room.

Miss Greer paused for a moment.

"For all of you," she said, "there remains the most important job of all. A job with the most responsibility of all. A job that requires your time and commitment and dedication."

"Like a chore?" asked another student.

"No," said Miss Greer. "Like an honor. You all have the job of getting informed and voting. It is serious and it is important, because it affects everyone.

"You are up to the job," she said. "But I don't think it is going to be easy. It's going to be a lot of work from everyone. What do you think?"

The class cheered again.

For the rest of the day, Miss Greer's class learned about elections and decided on rules. First, they decided that everyone in Miss Lila Greer's class would be included in the process. They were automatically registered to vote.

They would have a campaign, with rallies, posters, and speeches! After the campaigns, they would vote, and Miss Lila Greer's class at Blue River Creek Elementary would have the first democratically elected class pet in the history of the town.

CHAPTER 6

Sofia couldn't wait to tell Abuelo all the election news when she met him after school.

"I want to hear all about it," Abuelo said, "but let's wait for Marisella. I brought her some orejas."

Just then, Sofia's cousin waved and rolled over to them in her wheelchair. Abuelo gave her a hug and handed her a paper sack of baked treats.

"Are these for me, Abuelo?" she asked.

"You're a big sister now," said Abuelo. "That

deserves a special treat. And how is baby Mateo?"

Marisella's smile faded. "He sneezes all the time and has a rash," she said. "The doctor thinks it's allergies."

"Oh no," said Sofia.

"Mom made me put Pickles's birdcage in the laundry room so it's far from Mateo," said Marisella.

"He's allergic to your pet bird?" Abuelo asked.

"They're doing tests," said Marisella. "If he is, I'll have to get rid of Pickles." Her eyes teared up.

"I'm sorry," said Sofia, hugging her cousin.

Then—*BAM!*—an idea smacked Sofia right in the brain. What if Miss Greer's class adopted Pickles as their new pet? It would be perfect. Marisella could come visit Pickles any time she wanted, and Mateo would stop sneezing.

"Ooh!" said Sofia. "I have a great—"

Then—*BOOM!*—another idea struck. Bird

was one of the candidates for the election, and Sofia was the election commissioner. If she suggested Pickles for class pet, she could change the whole election. That wouldn't be fair to the Turtle supporters. Her entire job was making sure the election was fair. She had to be very careful about what she said and did. If she even told anyone about Pickles, it could make people change their vote. Anything an election commissioner did had to be for the good of the election, not a candidate.

A sinking feeling came over Sofia. How could she help Marisella and keep her promise to the class to be fair?

"Uh—" she said. "Well . . . Um."

"Are you okay, Sofia?" asked Abuelo. "You were going to tell us about your election."

"Maybe later," said Sofia quietly.

Abuelo gave Sofia his *I don't know what's going on but I'll change the subject* look.

"So, Marisella," said Abuelo in a big cheery voice. "Tell me all about this new baby. How are your parents? How is school?"

They headed down the sidewalk with Marisella answering questions, Abuelo munching a cookie, and Sofia feeling like her heart weighed a million, trillion tons.

CHAPTER 7

Sofia didn't see Marisella the next day and was so busy with the election that she stopped worrying about Pickles.

Every kid in Miss Greer's class found a way to get involved. Sofia's team would build a voting booth and make ballots. Some kids joined the Bird campaign with Rosie and some joined the Turtles with Ada. Some didn't join either campaign. They needed to know more before they made up their minds. Each campaign came up with catchy phrases to get people excited about their candidates. They put these slogans on posters and made buttons to wear.

Both Rosie and Ada tried to convince Sofia to tell the other kids that she supported their

candidates. But Sofia couldn't endorse Bird or Turtle like that. As election commissioner, she had a promise to keep. But even so, Ada and Rosie both stuck pins on Sofia's satchel when she wasn't looking. Sofia gave the buttons to Abuelo.

Abuelo's hat was covered with buttons from different causes he supported. He had been an activist for many years and always tried to help other people who were not being treated fairly. Abuelo believed that everyone could help, and it didn't matter if you were young or old.

Even though Sofia couldn't cheer for a candidate, she could still vote. She went back and forth trying to decide who to vote for. When she was younger, she'd had a turtle that had been her mother's. She'd loved it so much. It would be fun to have a turtle in the classroom every day.

On the other hand, voting for Bird might help Marisella.

Sofia didn't know what to do, so she was glad

when that Friday, Miss Greer suggested they make a class newspaper to explore the election in greater depth. It would be a good way to inform everyone about turtles and birds and how each might behave as a class pet. Sofia loved the idea of including news in their election. After all, the news played a big part in real presidential elections.

"A newspaper would be fun!" said Sofia.

"And important," said Miss Greer. "Our third president, Thomas Jefferson, said, 'The only security of all is in a free press.'"

"Our newspaper will be free?" asked Rosie.

"Yes," said Miss Greer. "But it could cost money."

"But then it wouldn't be a free press," said Iggy.

"A free press means that the government doesn't tell the paper what to print," said Miss Greer. "Reporters have freedom to write about whatever they want. That's important so we can always know what's going on."

"Shouldn't the government just tell us what's going on?" asked Ada.

"Usually," said Miss Greer. "But what if we elect a rotten apple? They wouldn't tell on themselves, would they? That's where the press can help."

"That sounds simple," said Sofia.

"There are many places in the world where it isn't," said Miss Greer. "Sometimes it's dangerous to report the news, and journalists have to be very brave. It's a tough job."

"We can do it!" said Rosie.

"I agree," said Miss Greer.

"This weekend," she added, "anyone who wants to can write an article. Or you could create a comic to show your opinion. That's called an editorial cartoon. They can be funny. And powerful. On Monday, we'll pull it all together into a newspaper!"

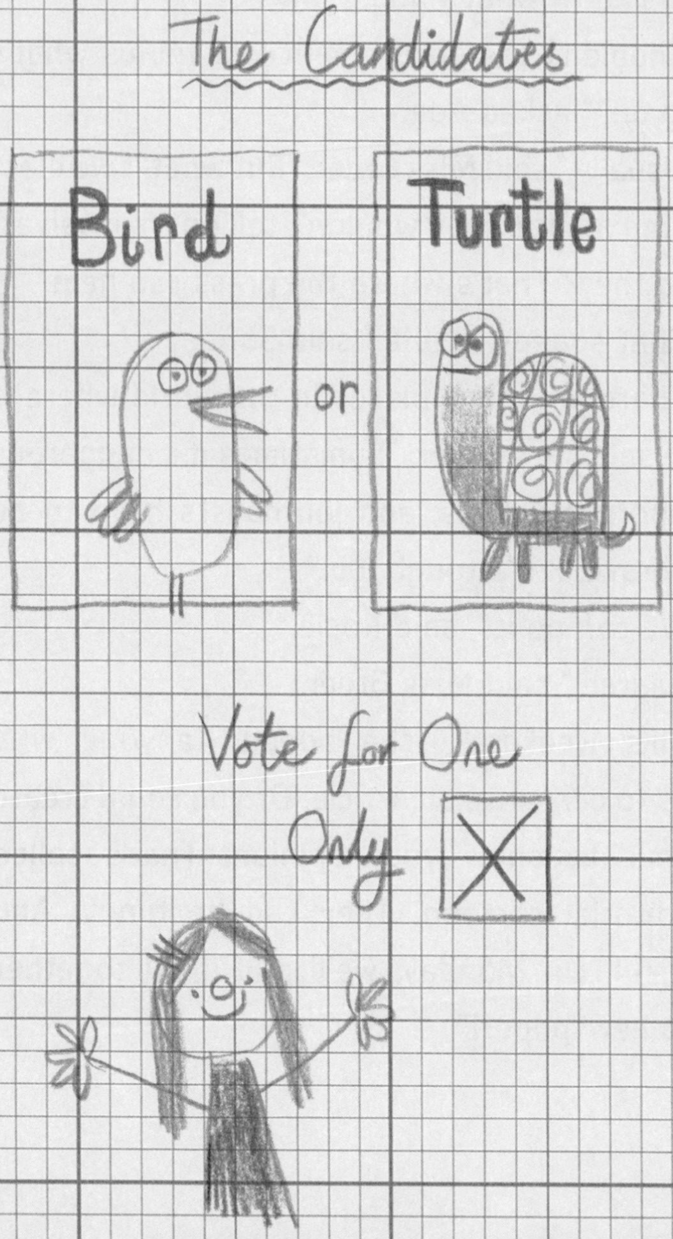
The Candidates
Bird
or
Turtle
Vote for One
Only

CHAPTER 8

Over the weekend, Sofia and her team worked on the voting booth, ballots, and signs encouraging everyone to vote. Each night, she drifted to sleep thinking about the election and her job to make sure it was all fair and square. She was feeling good about it. Maybe the class would be able to pick the best pet and the election would be as smooth as silk.

It was a great feeling.

Then, Monday morning, it all went *POOF!*

DON'T VOT

Turtles
are
so
Boring

SLOW
Boring
Don't vote Turtl

Don't get
SNAPPED!
BY
SNAPPY
TURTLES

Turtles
WHAT DO THEY
Do in their shells?
WHAT
are they
Hiding?

Turtles Smell!

Turtle
TERROR

CHAPTER 9

Miss Greer stared at the news stories. She did not look happy.

"This is not what I had in mind," she said.

"But you said we could write anything we wanted," said Rosie.

"Yes," said Miss Greer. "I did. But it has to be true. Look at this: *Birds evolved from dinosaurs! But are dinosaurs safe pets?*"

"That one is true," said Ada. "I read about it in my book on dinosaurs."

"But I didn't say we should get a dinosaur," said Rosie. "Just a little bird. That story makes birds sound scary and dangerous."

Rosie's cheeks flashed bright red. She frowned at Ada.

Ada frowned back.

"What about your picture?" asked Ada. She pointed to an illustration of a big snapping turtle with the caption "Turtle Terror!"

"Uncle Fred told me that snapping turtles could bite your finger off like an alligator!" said Rosie.

"We're not getting a snapping turtle!" said Ada.

"Turtles are as scary as alligators!" said someone in the back.

"Dinosaurs are scarier!" someone else replied.

Soon the whole class was arguing about dinosaurs and alligators. Sofia looked at her best friends, who stood frowning at each other. She had to do something. But what? She couldn't take either side without breaking her promise.

She thought about how Miss Greer got the class's attention by standing very still. Sofia stood perfectly still. Nobody noticed. Even Miss Greer was too busy trying to get Rosie and Ada to talk to each other to see what Sofia was doing.

The class got louder and louder.

Sofia tried clapping her hands in rhythm, like how Principal Howe did to get their attention at an assembly. Nobody noticed that either.

Sofia thought about Abuelo. He always told

her that when he saw a problem, he tried to help. He joined marches and organized people to change things. They used buttons and signs. Marches and letter writing. Sometimes, they quit buying products from companies that were not being fair to people. That was called a boycott, and it got people's attention.

They had another tool, too. A tool that got people's attention and helped them come together. That was exactly what the class needed now. Sofia lifted her head high. She cleared her throat. And she began to sing.

CHAPTER 10

If songs could unite marching protestors, they could unite classmates. Unfortunately, Sofia couldn't remember any of the songs Abuelo sang to her. She couldn't remember any songs that would inspire people to stop arguing and be kind. At that moment, she couldn't remember any songs at all.

Except one.

And so, Sofia Valdez sang the one song she

could remember. It was familiar. It was easy. It was also the most annoying song in the world.

"Old MacDonald had a farm. E-I-E-I-OOOOOO," Sofia started quietly. It felt weird to be the only one singing while everybody else was arguing. But she sang anyway.

She sang one verse. Then another. And another. With each verse, she sang a little louder. She added the hand motions she and Abuelo had learned at the library when she was little.

She zipped through the *OINK-OINK*s and the *QUACK-QUACK*s. She started on the *MOO-MOO*s. Sofia was on a roll.

She finished at full volume.

As the last note evaporated into the air, Sofia opened her eyes and realized for the first time how quiet a classroom could be when sixteen students and a teacher stood there staring at you with their mouths wide open.

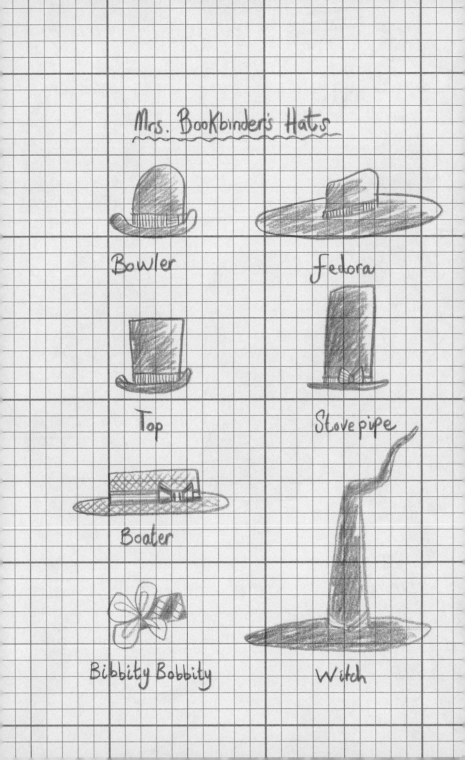

Mrs. Bookbinder's Hats

Bowler

Fedora

Top

Stovepipe

Boater

Bibbity Bobbity

Witch

CHAPTER II

Sofia's cheeks got hot, and she felt panicky inside.

"Uh . . ." she said. "I learned it at the library . . . Thought it might help . . . It was an emergency . . ."

She waited for the laughter to start. But there was no laughter. Instead, Miss Greer put her hand on Sofia's shoulder and smiled.

"Oh, Sofia!" said Miss Greer. "That's it!"

"That's what?" asked Sofia.

"An emergency!" said Miss Greer. "A library emergency!"

She left the room and returned with the school librarian, Mrs. Catherine Bookbinder.

Mrs. Bookbinder was one of Sofia's favorite people at Blue River Creek Elementary. She taught all the kids how to do research, and she read books with them. She helped them in the school makerspace, too. She was a great listener and always had the perfect book for everyone. Finding just the right book for just the right person at just the right time was Mrs. Bookbinder's superpower.

Mrs. Bookbinder also loved hats. She always had the right hat for the right occasion. Her hat collection hung on hooks around the entire library. At the moment, she wore a black fedora with a card stuck into the band. The card said PRESS.

"Miss Greer told me about your newspaper problem," she said. "I've got some great books and resources to help, but our public library has an amazing collection of papers you need to see. I've already talked to Mr. Page. He'll expect you this afternoon."

"Pack your snacks, class," said Miss Greer. "We're going on a field trip!"

Blue River Creek Library

Fido Dog-stoevsky   The Great Catsby

Reading
Buddies

CHAPTER 12

That afternoon, the class headed to the Blue River Creek Library. Sofia loved the library and went there often.

The public librarian, Mr. Page, was in a meeting, so they waited by some couches and beanbag chairs. Bee and Beau were there with a very tall, hairy dog and a calico cat. The animals wore red vests that said BLUE RIVER CREEK READING BUDDY.

Everyone knew Bee and Beau. They drove the recycling truck and volunteered at the fire department. Sometimes they brought specially trained pets to the library so kids could read stories to them. Today they had two pets Sofia hadn't met before.

"Hello!" said Bee, petting a lumpy spotted cat. "This is the Great Catsby!"

Catsby yawned and closed his eyes.

"He's thrilled to meet you," said Bee with a chuckle.

"Who is this?" asked Sofia, petting the large, long-haired dog next to Beau.

"This is Fido," said Beau. "His full name is Fido Dog-stoevsky. He's a Russian bookhound."

Fido nudged Iggy's hand.

"He wants you to read to him," said Beau. "He loves sad poetry."

"Where's Virginia Woof?" asked Sofia.

Virginia was a black dog who was as big as the beanbag chair and just as floppy. She loved it when Sofia leaned up against her and read stories.

"She's in the doghouse," whispered Beau. "She accidentally ate a book. Well, she slobbered on it, but Mr. Page is afraid Virginia will eat one."

"Afraid?" asked a tall, thin man who had appeared suddenly from behind a magazine rack.

"Who's afraid of Virginia Woof? Not I!" he said, scooting through the crowd of kids. "I welcome all our furry friends. Except when they eat the books! Same goes for kids!"

Mr. Page wore a black vest covered with bumpy pockets, and he held a large magnifying glass.

"Aha!" he said. "That reminds me of a quote from my favorite book."

He stuck his hand into one of the bumpy pockets and pulled out a teeny-tiny blue book titled *Famous Author Quotes*. It was the tiniest book Sofia had ever seen. He flipped the book open with his left thumb and held up the huge magnifying glass with his right hand.

"Here it is!" he said. He cleared his throat and read: "Outside of a dog, a book is man's best friend. Inside of a dog, it's too dark to read."

Mr. Page laughed. "Mark Twain was a smart one!" He stuck the book back into his pocket.

"Virginia Woof can come back," he said, "if she tries not to slobber so much." He scratched Fido's chin with a big smile. "But first, Mrs. Bookbinder phoned about your library emergency!"

He looked through his magnifying glass at the students. He carefully inspected each face. At last, he lowered the magnifying glass and nodded slowly.

"Hmm," he said. "It looks serious."

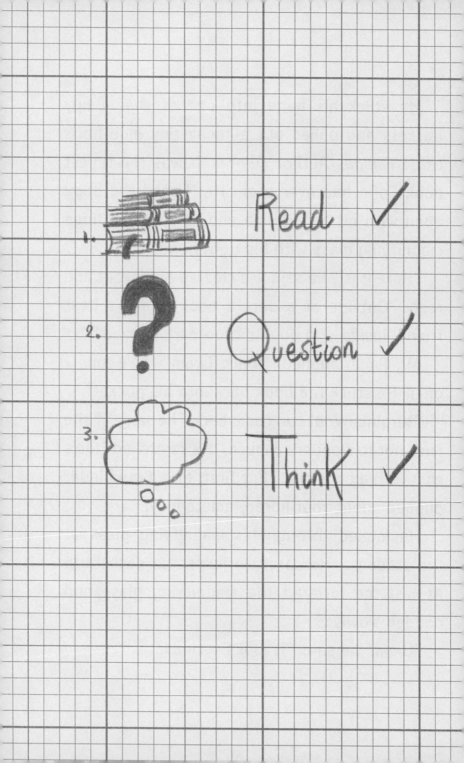

CHAPTER 13

"We had some trouble with our newspaper," said Miss Greer. "We're trying to write one with useful and accurate information for our readers. Perhaps you can help us."

"Aha!" said Mr. Page. "There's always help at the library!"

Mr. Page was an expert on newspapers. He led them through the town's collection. The archive had newspapers from Blue River Creek's earliest days.

"Newspapers have always helped shape our town and our country," he said. "Good journalism is like a flashlight into the darkness!

"A free press means that the government can't tell you what to write," he said. "That's important, because it means that the newspapers can tell the public when the government does something good *and* when it does something bad. It lets people know what's really going on. Without that, democracy gets in trouble." He reached into a pocket and pulled out a miniature green book. "This is my favorite book," he said, looking for a specific page.

"I thought the blue one was your favorite," said Sofia.

"That was my favorite book about author quotes," said Mr. Page. "This is my favorite book about reporting news. That's called *journalism*!

"Good journalism helps you understand all the facts," he said. "It has to be accurate and tell the good and bad parts of a story. That's the *news* part of the newspaper. But journalists also write editorials, where they share their thoughts on the news.

"And sometimes," he said, "people bend the news to show only their point of view. That's called *bias*. Sometimes they do it on purpose, but sometimes they don't even realize they're doing it."

"How can you tell what's what?" asked Sofia.

"Aha!" said Mr. Page, looking at Sofia through the magnifying glass. "That's it!"

"What?" asked Sofia.

"That," said Mr. Page, "is the most important question of all! No wonder they call you kids the Questioneers! You ask all the right questions!"

Mr. Page turned to leave.

"Wait!" cried Sofia. "You didn't answer the question! How can you tell when news is real?"

"Oh," said Mr. Page, wheeling around and

digging into his pocket. "That's in my favorite book!" He held up a tiny orange book with three words on the cover: READ. QUESTION. THINK.

"1. Read. Read everything," he said. "If you read from a wide variety of sources, you'll learn to spot bias. For instance, if you read ten stories and one leaves out important information or includes false statements, it will be obvious to you. Also, the more you read, the more you'll know about the topic. You'll get smarter, too.

"2. Question. Question everything," he said. "Ask questions and look for answers.

"3. Think," he said. "A lot of people forget to *think*, but it's the most important step. Always think. Nobody can do that one for you. And you know what else?"

"What?" asked the class.

"Here's what," he said. "Nobody can think for you, but nobody can think *like* you, either. You are the only person who thinks the way you do. Someday, there might be a problem, and you'll be the only person who can solve it. You've got to be ready for that."

Miss Greer nodded. "Read. Question. Think," she said. "That's good advice."

"And then . . ." said Mr. Page. "Do you know what you do?"

"What?" asked the class.

Mr. Page smiled. "You do it all over again! Read! Question! Think!"

"That's a lot of work," said Sofia.

"Aha!" said Mr. Page. "Isn't everything that's worth doing? Besides, there's always help at the library." He stuffed the orange book back into his pocket and pulled out a tiny black one. "And now, I leave you with a final question from my favorite book." He thumbed through the tiny pages.

"Where do library books like to sleep?"

"Where?" asked Ada.

"Beneath their covers!" said Mr. Page with a snort of laughter. "Oh geez. That's a good one!"

And with that, he ducked behind a bookshelf and was gone.

CHAPTER 14

After school, Sofia waited for Abuelo by the flagpole as always. Her brain was swimming with ideas from the field trip. She was deep in thought when suddenly she heard an angry voice behind her.

"Why didn't you tell me?"

She turned around. It was Marisella.

Sofia didn't have to ask what she meant.

"If you're in charge of the election," said Marisella, "you could tell everyone to vote for the bird! Then, if I have to give up Pickles, the class can take care of him! It solves everything!"

"I can't do that," said Sofia. "I can't tell people who to vote for. I have to be fair."

"It's not fair if I have to get rid of my pet and you won't help me," said Marisella. "You could if you wanted to."

Before Sofia could respond, Marisella turned her wheelchair and left.

A moment later, Abuelo arrived.

"I don't think I like being election commissioner," Sofia said. "No matter what I do, somebody will be mad at me."

"You can't fix how other people feel," said Abuelo. "All you can do is the right thing. Everything else will sort itself out."

Abuelo handed Sofia a warm cookie, and they walked home in silence.

What do Turtles EAT?
How to care for Birds
Talking with your Bird
How do you train a Turtle?
How to clean a Turtle
Famous Birds of the World
Best Bird Names

CHAPTER 15

The next morning, Miss Greer's classroom wall was covered with new articles from the class.

Miss Greer stood back and put her hands on her hips. She smiled.

"That's better!" she said, clapping her hands.

The newspaper was better, but things between Ada and Rosie were not. They weren't even speaking to each other. They were, however, very eager to talk to Sofia.

"Did you know that birds are hurt by the climate crisis?" Rosie whispered on her way to the pencil sharpener. "And bird populations are dropping around the world! We need to help them."

During spelling, Ada passed Sofia a note: *Did you know that turtles have existed for 215 million years? But some are going extinct!*

Then Rosie sent a note with a drawing of a flock of birds. Ada saw that, frowned, and sent another note with a picture of Sofia holding a turtle.

Before long, Sofia's pockets were stuffed with notes. Sofia was relieved when it was time for the class debate. She still didn't know who she was going to vote for, but at least the election would be over soon and things could get back to normal.

Rosie had brought Gizmo to add some interest to her presentation. Ada had borrowed a turtle named George from her cousin and had him in a small pen on the floor.

Ada and Rosie stood beside each other but didn't look at each other. Miss Greer introduced each of them, and their teams cheered. Then she called on Sofia to say a few words and ask some questions the class had written.

Sofia walked to the front of the class. She reached into her pocket and pulled out her folded speech. As she did, her friends' notes tumbled to the floor.

Sofia unfolded her speech and began to read. "We, the students in Miss Lila Greer's class, stand here today on the brink of a new era in Grade Two!" she began. "Never before has any class . . ."

She looked at the scraps of paper on the floor.

"Never before has any class . . ."

Sofia paused. She looked again at the scraps on the floor.

"Never . . ."

Suddenly, Sofia refolded her speech. She looked at Ada and Rosie and her classmates with their Bird and Turtle buttons. She looked at Miss Greer.

"Go ahead," said Miss Greer.

"My speech was fancy and talked about why elections are important and their history," Sofia said, "but I forgot something."

She took a deep breath and continued.

"Actually," Sofia said, "*we* forgot something.

"We forgot something important," she continued. "We got so excited about the election that we forgot why we're having one. Our election isn't about birds or turtles or pets at all. It's about deciding on something we care about *together*."

Sofia smiled. "*Together*," she said. "That's the important part.

"In a community, we have to care about each other and listen to each other," she continued.

"Otherwise, we won't want to be a community anymore, and it won't matter if we have a bird or a turtle. Or even if we have a pet at all.

"Well," Sofia finished quietly, "that's all I wanted to say."

The class burst into applause. Miss Greer nodded and smiled. Ada and Rosie looked at each other and then looked at Sofia. Then they squished in for a big hug.

"I'm sorry," whispered Rosie.

"Me too," whispered Ada.

They both hugged Sofia, who felt a big wave of relief wash over her. It was going to be okay after all. Rosie and Ada stepped out of the huddle and shook hands, and the debate began.

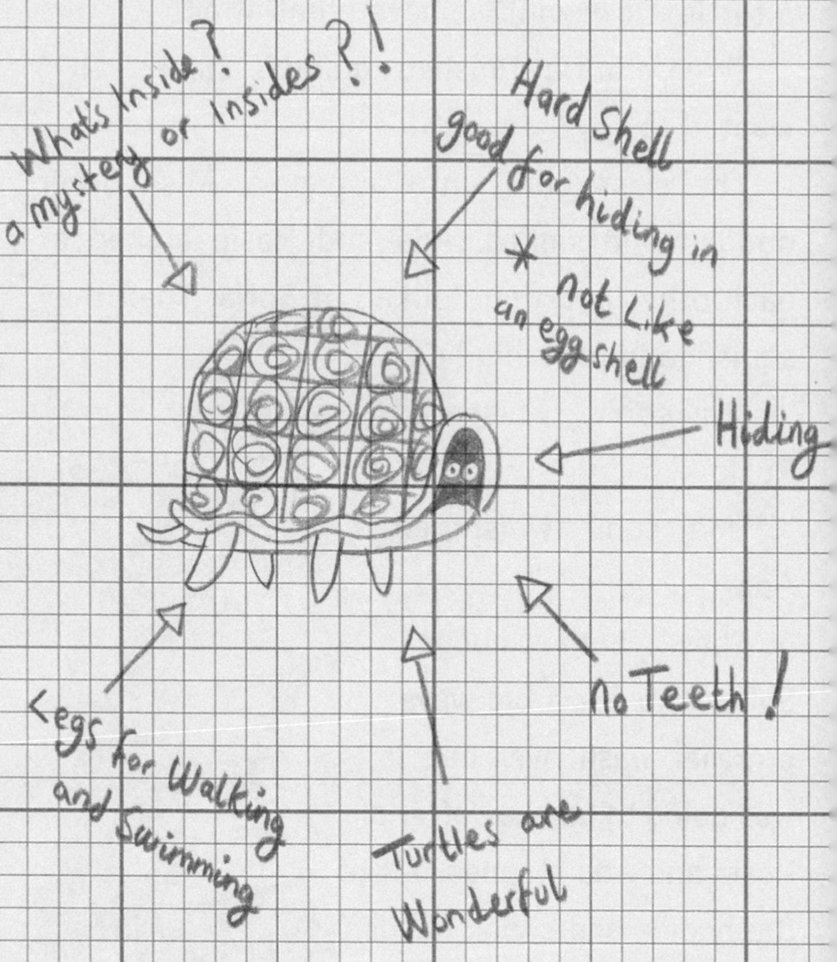
What's Inside?
a mystery or Insides?!
Hard Shell
good for hiding in
* not Like an egg shell
Hiding
no Teeth!
Legs for Walking and Swimming
Turtles are Wonderful

CHAPTER 16

T he first question goes to Ada," said Sofia.
"Why would a turtle be a good pet?"

Ada picked up George. "Just look at that face!"
she said.

The turtle pulled back its head and snapped
its shell shut.

"We can't even see its face!" said Rosie.

"I know!" said Ada. "Turtles are mysterious
and wonderful! What do turtles do in their
shells? How do they know when it's safe to come
out? How do they eat without teeth? There are

so many things to learn about them. Isn't that a good thing for a classroom pet?"

The class nodded.

"That's a good point," someone whispered.

Ada put the turtle back into the pen.

"Rosie," said Sofia. "Same question. Why would a bird make a good class pet?"

Rosie held her bird, Gizmo, on her finger.

"Birds make great pets," said Rosie. "Because they are beautiful and they can do something we could never do by ourselves: They can fly."

Gizmo lifted off her finger, looped around the room, and settled back onto her shoulder.

"We could learn a lot about flying by watching a bird in our classroom," she said. "And they sing, too."

Team Bird cheered. Team Turtle nodded.

The debate continued, with Sofia reading questions and Rosie and Ada answering in turns. Then they responded to each other's comments with questions or comments of their own. Sofia made sure they each had equal time to answer.

Each girl made her case before the voters. They talked about caring for the pets and what to expect from a pet bird or a pet turtle. The debate helped everyone understand what was involved with caring for birds and turtles.

At last, Ada and Rosie shook hands and sat down. The class cheered. Finally, it was time to vote. Though she couldn't tell anyone, Sofia had made up her mind. She knew which pet she wanted for the class.

Turtle ☐

Bird ☒

CHAPTER 17

Now, the moment we've all been waiting for," said Miss Greer. "Let the voting begin!"

Sofia wheeled the voting booth to the front of the room.

One by one, Sofia's classmates went into the booth, closed the curtain around it for privacy, and voted. As they came out, Sofia gave each student a special I VOTED sticker from Clerk Clark at City Hall.

When the voting was done, the vote counting began. Sofia opened the box and took out a ballot.

"Bird!" she said.

Miss Greer made a mark on the board in the Bird column.

Team Bird cheered.

"Turtle!" said Sofia, reading the next ballot.

Team Turtle cheered.

Sofia tallied the votes. At first, the Bird team led three votes to one. But soon, Turtle caught up. Then it took the lead.

Turtle—5

Bird—4

The voting continued. Once again, Bird took the lead, but not for long. Turtle caught up again.

Turtle reached eight votes. Bird had six.

"One more to win!" said Ada. "Go Turtle!"

"C'mon, Bird!" said Rosie.

Sofia pulled out the next vote.

"Bird!" she said. "Eight Turtle to seven Bird!"

She unfolded the next vote.

"BIRD!" she said again. "It's a tie! And the final vote will be the winner!"

The class stood up and eagerly watched as Sofia reached into the box for the final vote.

"The winner of the election," she said, "and our new class pet is . . ."

The class leaned closer.

Sofia felt around inside the box.

"Is . . ."

She opened the lid of the box and looked inside.

"Is . . ."

"Is?" asked Miss Greer.

A terrible look crossed Sofia's face.

"Is nobody!" she said.

She flipped the box upside down. Nothing fell out.

One vote was missing!

"It's been stolen!" someone yelled.

The class erupted into chaos.

"Thief! . . . It's unconstitutional! . . . Call the police! . . . Call Congress! . . . Call the president! . . . Call the free press!"

The confusion startled Gizmo. She flapped frantically around the room and landed on Miss Greer's hair.

"Good gracious!" said Miss Greer, trying to shoo Gizmo away. "Double dear me!" She twirled around and bumped into the turtle cage.

Gizmo flew to the tiptop of the window frame and chirped loudly while seventeen cheering

students and a flustered teacher tried to coax her down. Nobody noticed George make his escape down the hall.

It took the whole school the rest of the afternoon to find the turtle, who had fled all the way to the music room and hidden in the big bass drum.

Sofia left school angry and disappointed. She had worked hard to make sure the election went as smooth as silk, but instead it was bumpy as the bumpiest thing in the world. Sofia was so mad she couldn't even figure out what that was.

Abuelo watched Sofia as they walked home together. He could tell she didn't want to talk. He knew all of Sofia's expressions. This look told him she was thinking. They walked together silently. At last, they passed the library. They were almost home.

"I know just the thing for you," Abuelo said.

"What?" asked Sofia.

"You'll see."

CHAPTER 18

Sofia knew exactly what he meant when she walked in the door. Abuelo had started a batch of bread earlier that afternoon, and it was Sofia's job to knead the dough before it could rise again and be baked for dinner. Kneading dough was the best way in the world to get rid of a bad mood. As Sofia put on her apron and washed her hands, she told Abuelo about the voting catastrophe and the runaway turtle.

Abuelo tried to hide a laugh.

"It's not funny," said Sofia with a frown. Her cheeks burned, and she felt her anger rising.

"A runaway turtle is a little funny," said Abuelo. "Like a superhero! La Tortuga Rapida! Maybe she had jets in her shell!"

He was trying to cheer her up, but Sofia didn't want to be cheered up. She frowned harder.

Abuelo hugged her. "I'm sorry. You are right about the vanishing vote," he said. "That is very bad, Sofia. But the turtle? That is a little funny."

"Well," said Sofia. "Maybe a little. It was really fast!

"But what about the vote?" she asked. "I counted the ballots three times. It's gone! That makes me so mad!"

"Here you go," said Abuelo. "Give this a punch."

He dumped a puffy blob of bread dough onto the flour-covered counter in front of Sofia. She punched her fist into the warm dough. It

deflated like a thick, sticky balloon. She punched the dough again and again as hard as she could. Then she flopped the dough over and punched it some more. She picked the whole blob up and slapped it down on the counter, just like Abuelo had taught her to do.

WHAP! PUNCH! FLIP!

Sofia did it again.

WHAP!

"Who would steal a vote?" she asked.

PUNCH!

"Why would they do that?"

FLIP!

WHAP!

Sofia kneaded the dough as hard as she could. As she punched and pushed and pulled and flipped the dough, her anger melted away, and she felt calmer.

Abuelo dumped another bowl of dough onto

the counter beside Sofia and kneaded it quietly for a few minutes. Then he spoke.

"You know, I came to this country as a young man," he said softly. "I didn't speak much English, but I knew how to bake. My grandmother taught me just like I'm teaching you."

"Abuela Garces?" asked Sofia.

Abuelo nodded as he stretched the dough and flipped it over.

WHAP!

"It was a time when the migrant farmworkers were not treated right. They didn't get paid enough to feed their families," he said. "They didn't have good water to drink or good housing. But they were growing food for the whole country. The *whole* country! Imagine that! It wasn't fair. So they decided to do something."

"What did they do?" asked Sofia.

THWAP!

"They got everybody to stop eating grapes," he said.

"That would be easy," said Sofia. "I don't like grapes."

"It was very hard," said Abuelo, giving her his *you need to eat more fruit* look.

"People love grapes," he said. "But liking grapes was not the point. The strikers got the whole country to stop buying grapes so the companies would pay attention and treat the workers better."

"Did it work?" asked Sofia.

"Yes!" said Abuelo with a smile. "It did. But it was very hard and took a long time. I wasn't a farmworker, but I was mad about how they were treated. It was not fair or right. Then I remembered what Abuela Garces had told me. And I'm going to tell it to you." He looked straight at Sofia. "She told me, 'Mijo, take your anger and make something good from it.' So I did!"

"What did you make?" asked Sofia.

"Bread," said Abuelo. "I found a job in a grocery store, and I saved my money and bought flour and butter. Every night, I went home after work and I baked. I took all my anger and used it to make the dough soft and delicious. Just like you are doing now. I made pan dulce and orejas and bread and all the things Abuela had taught me. Then I took them to the families of the striking workers who needed it."

"Did they like it?" asked Sofia.

"Of course!" said Abuelo with a wink. "You've tasted my baking! And you know, some of those people became friends, and still are! There is always a way to help, Sofia. You just have to figure it out.

"Mad can be a bad thing," he went on. "And mad can be a good thing. What you do with it decides."

They worked in silence for a few minutes, kneading their dough until it was smooth and soft. Then they shaped the dough into evenly-sized rolls and put them into a buttered pan to rise once more before baking.

"I know what I'm going to do," said Sofia, rolling the last bit of dough into a ball. "I'm going to find out who stole the vote!

"But first," she added. "I have just the thing for you, Abuelo."

Sofia pulled, pinched, and squished the dough. At last, she handed her creation to Abuelo.

"It's the world's newest superhero!" she said. "La Tortuga Rapida!"

"A hero for the times," said Abuelo. "Or at least for dinner."

CHAPTER 19

The next morning, everyone was talking about the stolen vote and the runaway turtle.

"Yesterday did not go as we had planned," Miss Greer said. "It was rather stressful, but I think it will be okay. Like I said to myself this morning, 'Lila, those shoes don't match!' But that's not important. The other thing I said to myself was 'Democracy is important, and we will figure this thing out!' So today we will learn what we can and go from there. Like Rosie says, 'The only true failure can come if we quit.'"

The class cheered.

Miss Greer continued, "Before we start, let's do one final search to see if that ballot can be found."

They searched high and low for the vanishing vote.

The ballot did not turn up. Finally, Miss Greer called off the search. They would put the election aside for a day. She asked Sofia to research what happens when there is a tie in other elections.

After that, they turned to reading, spelling, and math, but Sofia couldn't focus. She couldn't stop thinking about the vanishing vote—and how she'd noticed that one person had sat reading a book while everyone else hunted for it.

At last, it was recess. The class left the room and headed down the hall toward the playground. Sofia heard laughter and squeals of joy as her friends burst out the door and onto the playground. But with each step, her heart grew heavier and heavier. At last, she stepped onto the playground and stood with a sad look on her face as she watched one student swinging happily back and forth on the swings.

"Oh, my friend," she said quietly. "What have you done?"

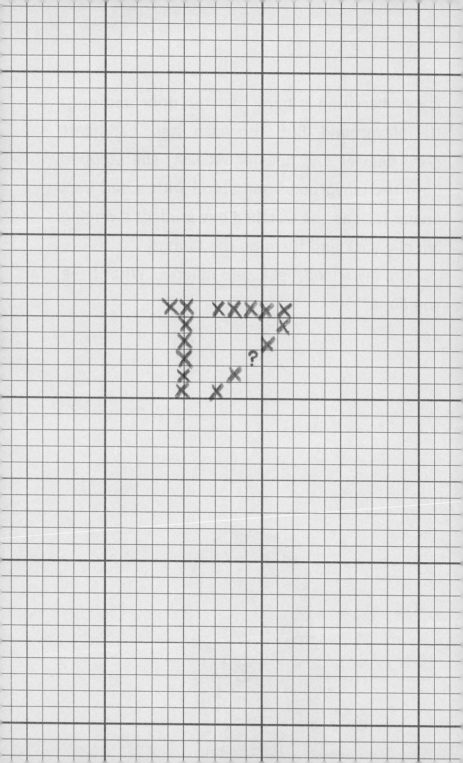

CHAPTER 20

Sofia took a deep breath and walked to the swings.

"Hi, Sofia!" said Iggy, jumping off the swing and landing next to her.

"You shouldn't have done it," said Sofia.

"It's okay," said Iggy.

"No, it's not!" said Sofia angrily.

"I wasn't swinging high when I jumped," said Iggy. "I didn't get hurt."

"Not that," said Sofia. "I know you stole the vote!"

Iggy was shocked. "I did not!" he said. "I'm not a thief. I didn't steal the vote."

"Then why didn't you help look for it with everyone else?" she asked. "I think you knew we wouldn't find it because you already had it!"

"That's good detective work," said Iggy. "But you're wrong. I didn't steal the vote."

Sofia looked at him suspiciously.

"I didn't steal the vote," Iggy continued, "because there wasn't a vote to steal!"

"What?" asked Sofia. "Seventeen people went into the booth and voted."

"No," said Iggy. "Seventeen people went into the booth, but only sixteen voted. I didn't vote."

"Why not?" asked Sofia.

"I like turtles and birds," said Iggy. "They are both like architects. Turtles grow their own houses on their backs, and birds make houses from sticks. But more than that, I like Rosie and Ada. They're both my friends, and I don't want

either of them to be upset. So I just let other people vote."

Sofia frowned. "Why didn't you say something when we were looking for the ballot?" she asked.

"I was going to . . ." said Iggy, "but everybody was mad about the vanishing vote, and I felt embarrassed. And I figured other people knew more about the pets anyway, because I wasn't paying much attention during the debates. I was building a tiny igloo out of paper wads."

"Iggy!" said Sofia.

"I know," said Iggy. "But it was inspired by the turtle's shell."

Sofia shook her head. "It's everybody's job to know what's going on," she said.

"I know. I'm sorry about the ballot," said Iggy. "But if it helps, I think you're a good election commissioner, and I know you'll figure out what to do."

CHAPTER 21

On the walk home from school, Sofia kicked a small stick off the sidewalk. Pup fetched it and brought it back to her. Sofia scowled and threw the stick. Pup brought it back. This continued all the way home.

"Iggy didn't vote, Abuelo!" said Sofia. "Everybody should vote! It's important."

"It is," said Abuelo, "but a person doesn't have to vote if they don't want to. That's a right, too.

Iggy thought he was doing a good thing letting others decide."

"Not voting makes as big a difference as voting," said Sofia. "Iggy thought he would let somebody else take care of it, but because he did that, we have a tie."

"People don't think one vote makes a difference," said Abuelo, "but it does. Every single one. If a person doesn't vote, they give up their power to change things. Worse than that, they give that power to somebody else, who might not use it the way they want."

"It's too late now," said Sofia.

Abuelo gave her a hug.

After dinner, they went to the library to learn how election ties could be broken.

"Hold the door, Sofia!" called a familiar voice.

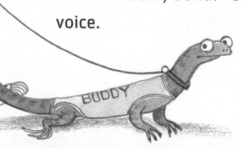

Sofia looked behind her. Bee was carrying a black duck. Beau followed her with a large lizard on a leash. Both animals wore Reading Buddy vests.

"Meet our newest Reading Buddies!" said Bee. "Moby Duck."

QUACK!

"And the Lizard of Oz," said Beau. "We're expanding our program. Wait until you meet Hamlet!"

"He's a pig," said Bea. "But he loves books!"

"Who doesn't?" said Mr. Page. "How can I help you? You know there's always help at the library!"

Sofia told him about the election, and Mr. Page led her to a section of the library filled with books about elections.

Sofia learned that each election's rules depend on where the election is held. Some election ties lead to a whole new election. Sometimes, one official picks the winner. Sometimes they decide with a coin toss. One time, a whole state senate was tied, and one seat would decide which party had the power to make laws. The senate seat election was tied, too! The governor flipped a coin to decide who would win the seat and which party would control the state.

"I bet a lot of people in that state wish they had voted," said Mr. Page.

Before Sofia could respond, Moby Duck waddled by.

"That reminds me," said Mr. Page, pulling a tiny book from his pocket. "What time do ducks wake up?"

"I don't know," said Sofia.

"At the quack of dawn!" said Mr. Page with a belly laugh. "Oh golly. That's a good one."

He walked away chuckling.

Sofia smiled weakly. She wasn't in the mood for jokes. Even good ones. She stared at her notes and sighed. Her research had turned up a lot of information about tied elections. In the end, she had four ideas, but she didn't know which the class would choose, and she wasn't sure she liked any of them. As election commissioner, though, it was her job to help the class figure it out. She and Abuelo left the library and headed home.

Tied Election Ideas

1. Miss Greer decides.
2. Vote again.
3. Flip a coin.
4. Call the whole thing off.

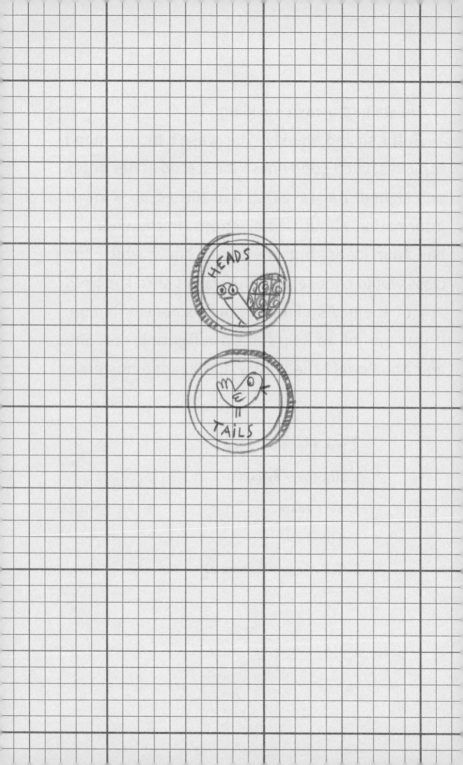

CHAPTER 22

Sofia had thought all night about what she was going to say to the class. She didn't want to tell them that Iggy didn't vote. Voting was secret. So she figured that not voting should be secret, too.

Toward the end of the school day, Miss Greer asked Sofia about the tiebreaker. Sofia presented what she'd learned about tied elections. Then, as election commissioner, she asked the other students what they wanted to do. Nobody wanted to call off the election. Only two students wanted to redo the entire election. Twelve liked the coin toss because they thought it was more exciting. Two people wanted Miss Greer to decide.

"No," said Miss Greer. "This election is yours to decide. Not mine."

In the end, the class agreed on the coin toss. Miss Greer handed Sofia a shiny quarter.

"As election commissioner," she said, "you should toss the coin."

Sofia took a deep breath.

"Heads is Turtle," she said. "Tails is Bird!"

Sofia balanced the quarter on her thumbnail for a moment, then flicked as hard as she could. The coin twirled up, up, up into the air and then tumbled down, down, down into Sofia's open palm. As soon as it hit her right palm, Sofia slapped the coin onto the back of her left hand. The class leaned forward. All eyes were on Sofia's hands. Miss Greer held her breath.

At last, Sofia pulled back her hand and revealed the coin.

"Heads!" she said. "The class pet is a turtle!"

Team Turtle cheered! Iggy cheered.

"Rats!" said someone from Team Bird.

"Congratulations, Ada," said Rosie, holding out her hand.

"Thank you, Rosie!" said Ada.

They shook hands. Soon, the class was talking about a good name for a turtle and how to raise money to buy one. They decided to name the new turtle after the author of *Frankenstein*. Her name was Mary Shelley. Everyone cheered.

The bell rang. Sofia slowly packed her backpack and headed out of school, dreading the walk home. She knew she had to tell Marisella that Miss Greer's class was getting a new pet.

And it wasn't going to be Pickles.

?

Brainstorm

My House ✗　　City Hall

Pet Shop ✗　　The Library

The Zoo ✗

The park ?

CHAPTER 23

Marisella was talking with Abuelo by the flagpole when Sofia, Rosie, Ada, and Iggy came out. She took one look at Sofia's face and knew what had happened.

"I'm sorry, Marisella," said Sofia. "I voted for Bird, but Turtle won. Maybe Mateo is not allergic to birds and it will be okay."

Marisella's eyes filled with tears. "He's allergic," she said.

"Oh no!" said Sofia. "Can we keep Pickles, Abuelo?"

"Oh, no, love," said Abuelo. "Do you remember what happened when we kept him for a week last year?"

Sofia and Abuelo had kept Pickles while Marisella's family went on vacation. Pup didn't stop barking for a week. Pickles was a nervous wreck when he got back to Marisella.

"Pup and I will keep you company on your way home," Abuelo said to Marisella, whose tears were streaming down her cheeks. "I'll see you at home, Sofia."

Sofia nodded.

Pup jumped onto Marisella's lap and they headed down the sidewalk with Abuelo.

"I didn't know that Marisella's pet bird might need a home," said Iggy. "I would have voted for a bird if I had."

"I couldn't tell you," said Sofia.

"What can we do to help?" asked Ada.

The Questioneers walked and brainstormed as they went. They reached the steps of City Hall but had no ideas.

"I feel so bad for Pickles and Marisella," said Rosie. "I wish somebody could help."

Sofia nodded. Abuelo had said there was always a way to help, but what could they do?

They sat there for a few minutes when suddenly Sofia looked at the building next to City Hall. It was the library. She jumped up.

"That's it!" said Sofia. "There's always help at the library! I know what to do!"

Sofia told them her plan. Each person had something to do to help. Rosie, Ada, and Iggy took off together. Sofia ran straight to the library, pulled open the massive door, and went inside.

CHAPTER 24

Sofia found help at the library. And it was speedy. Thirty minutes later, she met Iggy, Ada, and Rosie at Marisella's house. Marisella was on the porch with Pickles.

"We're just playing together a little more," said Marisella. "Mom is taking him to the pet store tomor—" Her voice cracked and she blinked back tears.

"We're sorry the class didn't vote for a bird," said Rosie.

"Me too," said Marisella. "But I understand."

"I think we all understand better now," said Iggy.

Sofia smiled at her friend. "We do," she said.

"I have to go pack up Pickles's stuff," said Marisella.

"Wait!" said Sofia. "We have a surprise! Close your eyes."

Marisella closed her eyes, and the Questioneers got ready.

"Okay!" they called. "Ta-daaa!"

Marisella opened her eyes. She was stunned.

"What?" she asked. "I don't understand. How could—"

"Sofia went to the library and asked," said Iggy.

"You mean—" started Marisella.

"Yep!" said Sofia. "He can start as soon as you want. And you can visit anytime!"

"Thank you!" said Marisella, admiring her beautiful new Reading Buddy.

"Pretty bird!" squawked Pickles. "Meow! Woof!"

"Smart bird," said Sofia. "You'll fit right in."

"I think he will!" said Marisella. "Thanks to you."

"Do you think the Reading Buddies could visit school, too?" asked Rosie. "They could help even more kids learn to read!"

Sofia smiled. She loved how good ideas grew into more good ideas when people worked together. She also loved her friends, who were always ready to help.

After a few minutes, Marisella went inside. Ada and Rosie walked down the sidewalk together, but Iggy stayed back a moment.

"Thank you, Sofia," he said. "You helped Marisella and everybody."

"We all helped," said Sofia with a smile.

Iggy smiled back. "I was wondering," he said. "What do you think about a class mascot? We could have another election to vote on it!"

Sofia smiled. "Like the Lions?" she asked. "Or the Bears?"

"I was thinking something more like the Chrysler Buildings!"

Sofia grinned. "Gets my vote."

The two friends parted ways. Sofia smiled as she thought about Marisella and her parrot and Iggy and his vote. Even though it hadn't gone as she had imagined at the beginning, the process had worked. They still had to raise money for the class turtle, and there was lots to do. She thought about Miss Greer, who had been nervous about trying something new and electing a class pet. It really had been a Learning Experience.

Sofia reached into her satchel and pulled out a cookie. She took a bite and smiled.

Abuelo had been right, too. The election had been a Learning Experience. But, like this batch of cookies, it was a good one.

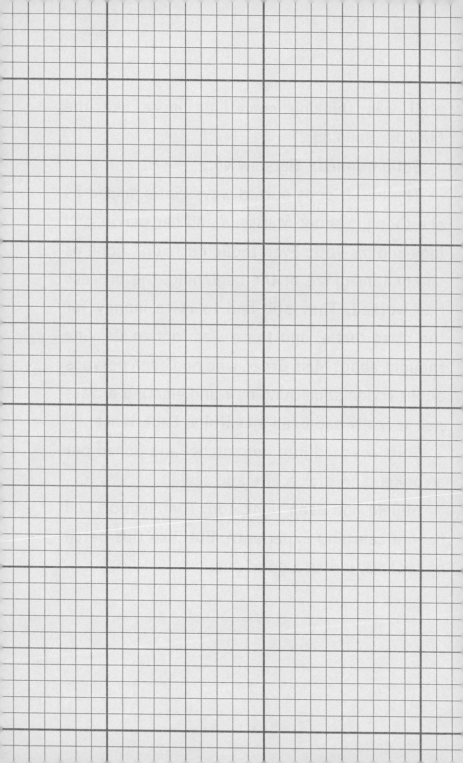

I DON'T WANT TO VOTE!

"*I don't want to vote!*" Jack said to Jill.
"*One vote doesn't matter, and it never will.*
The Fat Cats get fatter. The powers that be
don't give a nickel for people like me."

Jill simply nodded a moment or two.
"Yep," she responded. "What can you do?"
Election Day came. Jack stayed home in bed,
and the Fat Cats got fatter, just like he'd said.

Jill, however, showed up to vote,
and her vote REALLY counted. It's worth
     taking note.
It turns out that Jill didn't care about Jack
or his healthcare or clean air
or water or education or the arts
or housing or justice
or free and fair elections
or the planet . . . or . . .

. . . Well, it's safe to say
she cared about Jill, and she got her way.
But it turns out—in one thing—Jack was
     quite right.
His vote didn't matter!
Because he quit the fight.

DELANO GRAPE STRIKE

On September 7, 1965, farmworkers in Delano, California, began a strike against the grape growers. They were led by a man named Larry Itliong.

The strikers were migrant workers, most of whom came from the Philippines. Two weeks later, the Mexican migrant workers joined the strike. They were led by Dolores Huerta and Cesar Chavez. The workers wanted contracts that would ensure better working conditions. The grape growers refused.

The migrants toiled in terrible conditions from sunrise to sunset without rest. They had no toilets in the fields where they worked or cold water to drink as they labored beneath the burning sun. Their families were poor and lived in terrible conditions, often without good food for their families. For their hard work, they earned only about seventy cents per hour.

The Filipino and Mexican workers joined

forces to form a union called the United Farm Workers. The workers marched and protested. Dolores Huerta created a slogan to inspire them: Sí, Se Puede! It means "Yes, it can be done!"

The strike was difficult and dangerous. Workers were sometimes met with violence from local authorities or arrested. Even so, they used nonviolent resistance and community organizing to tell people about their cause. The strike lasted for years, but the grape growers would not agree to contracts for the workers.

The strike organizers and workers came up with a new idea. They called for a boycott. They asked people around the country to stop buying and eating grapes unless they were picked by union workers. Over seventeen million people listened and stopped buying grapes. Finally, in July 1970, the grape growers agreed to contracts, and the strike ended. The strike revolutionized the farm labor movement in America.

PICKING A PRESIDENT

It takes a long time to elect an American president. Candidates spend months or even years trying to build support and raise money. Candidates come from many different backgrounds and various careers, but most have been elected to a state or national office before becoming president. They are usually members of a political party.

The United States has two main political parties: Democratic and Republican. There are other smaller parties that are known as third parties. An Independent candidate is one who is not bound by or committed to a political party.

Only one person can be president. However, many people will want to try. Each presidential election starts with many candidates trying to become the favorite of their political party. Candidates crisscross the country to show that they care about the local people. They hold rallies. They seek attention from the media. They participate in televised debates with their fellow candidates to discuss important issues and clarify their positions. They also spend a lot of time asking for money, because elections are very expensive.

Candidates hire people to help them. Also, supporters volunteer to help. Campaign staff and volunteers try to get people excited about their candidate, register voters, and help people get to their voting place.

Each political party picks its candidate through a set of statewide elections. For their elections, each state uses one of two systems: primaries and caucuses.

- **Primary:** Party members go to a polling place and vote for their candidate.

- **Caucus:** Party members meet locally to discuss and vote and discuss and vote and repeat the process until they decide on the candidate they want.

During the Primary season, candidates of the same party challenge each other. Sometimes they are tough on each other. They are trying to sway voters to pick them as the party nominee over their competition.

Each party has a national convention, where members from each state meet to pick the presidential candidate. Conventions are gigantic events with speeches, funny hats, signs, more speeches, singing, voting, more speeches, more funny hats, more speeches, and balloons! And speeches! So many speeches!

Finally, the party candidate is nominated. Everyone in the party gathers to support that person against the other party's nominee, and the general election begins!

GENERAL ELECTION BEGINS!

The General Election is the final push toward election day. At this point, there are only two main candidates: one from each major party. The candidates spend the fall traveling the country trying to get people excited to vote for them. There are debates, rallies, speeches, news interviews, and other events to get attention for the candidate.

News organizations and other media outlets spend an enormous amount of time trying to figure out who will win the race. Voters might be interested in this horse-race view of the election, but information on the candidates' records and ideas are more important. Voters must get informed to understand the issues and what each candidate might do if elected.

JOURNALISM

Journalism is the act of gathering and sharing information about things that happen. Journalists tell us the "who, what, when, where, why, and how" of events. Journalists share their findings in print, online, on TV, on the radio, and in other formats.

The United States has a free press, which means that the government cannot control or influence what is reported. A free press acts like a watchdog and helps citizens know when its officials are doing their jobs well and when they are not. It can even reveal abuses of power or illegal actions.

Journalism and a free press are essential to a thriving democracy.

A journalist's job is to report the truth. That means accurately reporting facts. They must make sure the facts can be proven. Journalists also give facts a context so people can understand them. Journalists have a responsibility to point out errors, missing information, and even lies from leaders. The loyalty of journalists is to the readers, not to the people who pay their salaries or print their work or who have political power or other kinds of power.

There are many kinds of journalists. All base their work on verifiable facts and make an honest effort to analyze those facts.

- Reporters collect facts and report stories.

- Columnists explain their point of view on a topic.

- Editorial cartoonists use art and often humor to express an opinion of a news event.

- Editorial writers express the views of the publication on a topic.

News sources that uphold the principles of good journalism help citizens to understand what is happening. However, not all sources that claim to be news sources do this. Some distort the truth or spread false information. They can do this by reporting incorrect information or by leaving out important details.

Being a journalist is hard work. It can also be dangerous work. In many countries, a journalist who disagrees with the government or who reports on the government's bad actions can be attacked or thrown in prison or worse. Freedom of the press is a right that can be lost if it is not protected.

Democracy danger: Pay attention when politicians call journalists bad names because they do not like the stories that are reported. Ask yourself why the politician is trying to make people doubt the story. Do your research. Are the reporters doing their jobs and using evidence? Do other credible news outlets confirm the reporting?

Democracy danger: Beware of anyone who calls the free press the "enemy of the people." These words have been used by tyrants for centuries. They are powerful and dangerous words meant to make people stop trusting facts. **Once the people stop believing facts, they are easy to fool. People who are easily fooled are easily taken advantage of by bad leaders. That is when democracy fails. That is when fear and violence govern instead of laws. Always be suspicious of a leader who says this!**

HOW TO SPOT AND STOP FAKE NEWS

- Check who created the content before believing it or sharing it. Is it a real person or group known to share valid information? Are they credible? If the information is from a group or website, figure out who they are. What is their mission?

- Check the date. An old story might not be fake, but it might not have all the current helpful information, either. Having current, credible information is important.

- Read more than the headline of a news story. Headlines grab your attention, but they don't always match the content of the article. **People who spread wrong opinions based only on headlines add to public confusion.**

- Is the story confirmed by other credible news sources? Most news stories are reported first by one news outlet, but soon, if the story is based on fact, other outlets will confirm the story themselves and report on it, too. They may even add additional facts and details they discovered during their confirmation of the story. If you cannot find several credible news sources to confirm a story, it might not be true. Does your source give supporting links or resources? Are they valid? Can you find other credible sources by doing some research?

- These nonpartisan websites can help you to fact-check news stories:

  Factcheck.org: Fact-checks what is said by politicians, TV ads, interviews, press releases, and more.

  Politifact.com: The site's Truth-O-Meter ranks the statements of politicians from "True" to "Pants on Fire"!

Snopes.com: Checks facts on many wild "fake news" stories.

- Remember that a political meme is someone's attempt to sway you. Not to inform you.

- Is it satire? Satire is a type of comedy that uses wit, irony, or sarcasm to mirror the actual news. Sometimes it's hard to tell the difference.

- Read many, many sources and compare how they cover the same story. Think about how the reports differ and what those differences might reveal about the news sources. Reading widely will help you figure out which sources are trying to sway you with false information or by leaving out important details.

GET OUT THE VOTE!

Voting is a right but also a big responsibility. Voters should prepare to vote by becoming informed about topics that affect them and their families, communities, states, countries, and planet. Also, voters should learn about the experience and records of candidates, as well as the candidates' plans for the country if they are elected. Remember: *Read. Question. Think!*

While we elect others to hold office, helping your country is *everyone's* job. It is serious and important and demands from each of us our best and most courageous selves.

Our elections and our democracy only work when EVERYONE gets informed and gets involved.

WHY VOTE?

There are many important reasons to vote:

- Voting has consequences. Voting gives you a say in what happens in your community/city/state/country. Elections can even affect the planet! You must be informed and vote wisely.

- Not voting has consequences. If you don't vote, you give up your power to make change. AND you give your power to the people who do vote. Can you be sure they want the same things you want—or need?

- Voting honors those who fought for your right to vote. History is filled with people who struggled, sacrificed, and even died for your right to vote. Respect that.

- Even if an election doesn't affect you directly, the outcome could be very important to others in your community. Get informed and think about how your vote could help children or the homeless or any other group that might not have a voice. Your vote can make a difference in their lives. Use your power to help them.

- Even if you are too young to vote now, you will be old enough very soon. Prepare now by learning all you can about your community, city, state, country, and planet. Make a habit of getting informed. Seek out reliable news sources every day. Read. Question. Think. That's your job.

Democracy is complicated. It is difficult. It is exciting and it is powerful. Democracy is also fragile. It depends on each of us doing our best to protect it. Democracy depends on each of us getting informed and staying informed. It depends on each of us getting involved and staying involved. Always.

Democracy is not somebody else's job.

It is your job. You do it by knowing what is going on in your community, city, state, country, and planet and doing what you can to make it better. It is hard work. But it is how you can help others. It is how you can make a difference.

Read! Question! Think!

And remember . . . there is always help at the library!

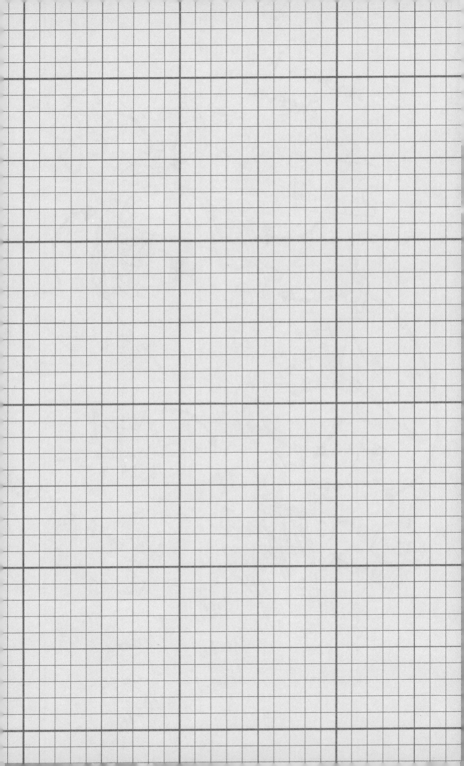

ABOUT THE AUTHOR

ANDREA BEATY is the bestselling author of the Questioneers series, as well as many other books, including *Dorko the Magnificent, Secrets of the Cicada Summer, Attack of the Fluffy Bunnies,* and *Happy Birthday, Madame Chapeau.* She has a degree in biology and computer science and spent many years in the computer industry. She now writes children's books in her home outside Chicago.

ABOUT THE ILLUSTRATOR

DAVID ROBERTS has illustrated many books, including the Questioneers series, *The Cook and the King,* and *Happy Birthday, Madame Chapeau.* He lives in London, where, when not drawing, he likes to make hats.

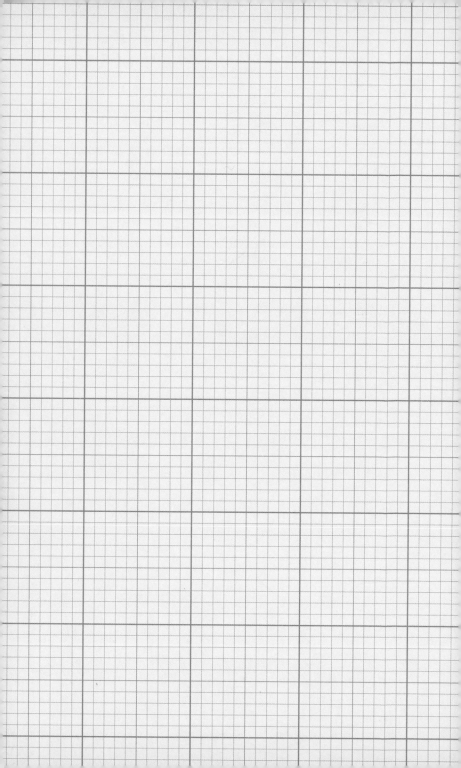